CSI: Classroom

Written by Frank Pedersen
Illustrated by James Hart

Contents

1	Something Fishy	4
2	Suspect Evidence	14
3	A Conspiracy	23
4	The Plot Thickens	34
5	Guilty!	44

NELSON
CENGAGE Learning™
For learning solutions, visit cengage.com.au

Meet the Characters

Dwayne Pipe

A classroom crime-scene investigator.

Shandy Lear

A classroom crime-scene investigator.

Louden Clear

A classroom crime-scene investigator.

Barb Dwyer

A teacher (and suspect).

Seymour Leggs

A principal (and suspect).

Janitor John

A janitor (and suspect).

Dear Reader

Everyone likes to watch TV crime shows, where teams of highly trained investigators solve impossible crimes. Crime-scene investigation, or CSI, requires attention to detail, some lucky breaks and some very colourful characters who seem to say hilarious things, even when they're trying to be serious. It's the perfect recipe for a book, just like this!

Frank Pedersen

Author

The Crime Scene

1. A bookcase (the victim's usual place of residence)
2. The deceased's final location
3. The teacher's hideout (AKA "her desk")
4. Classroom desks (deserted, no witnesses)

1 Something Fishy

Lifeless, the body sprawled at a crazy angle across the carpet, surrounded by a damp stain. A single accusing eye stared sightlessly at Dwayne Pipe.

Dwayne whisked off his sunglasses and, with a grim look, knelt down beside the victim to investigate. Reaching out a hand, he touched the victim.

"Just as I initially suspected," he murmured, consulting his wristwatch and carefully noting the time. Then Dwayne dialled a familiar combination on his mobile phone.

"Dwayne," answered a female voice. "What's happening? What's wrong?"

"Shandy," growled Dwayne. "What's happening is something altogether fishy. Assemble the investigation team. Right away." Dwayne heard Shandy Lear, his premier forensic assistant, gasp.

"I'm heading there immediately," said Shandy, breaking the connection.

Delicately, Dwayne Pipe picked up the recently deceased goldfish and, with his remaining hand, replaced his sunglasses on his nose.

He surveyed the classroom, knowing its empty furniture would soon be filled with students, inadvertently contaminating important forensic evidence. His detached professional eye completed the preliminary examination. The bookcase, where the goldfish bowl had until now been kept, seemed relatively undisturbed, apart from a puddle of greenish water. Above the bookcase, the classroom's air conditioning vent was blowing a steady stream of cool air. Below, a solitary book lay on the floor. Dwayne examined it closely for fingerprints and, finding none, replaced it on the bookshelf. His carefully trained eye kept returning to the upturned goldfish bowl, and he noticed a fateful sign on the wall that someone had written during a classroom project.

"Fish are cold blooded," declared the sign.

"They certainly are," nodded Dwayne in grim agreement. "And this, therefore ... is a cold-blooded crime."

Beneath a canopy of eucalyptus trees, the gleaming bicycle sped towards the school, twisting and turning to avoid the possum droppings littering the asphalt cycleway. Gripping the handlebars tightly, Louden Clear impatiently manouevred his bicycle past other unsuspecting riders pedalling towards Gandwilli School. The urgent text message received from his colleague, Shandy Lear, had alerted him that he had to get to school before the other kids that morning.

Louden Clear stared at the text message the instant his mobile phone bleeped. What could Shandy mean? Then it dawned on him. No matter which way he looked at it, the message could only mean one thing. He really did have to get to school before the other kids that morning.

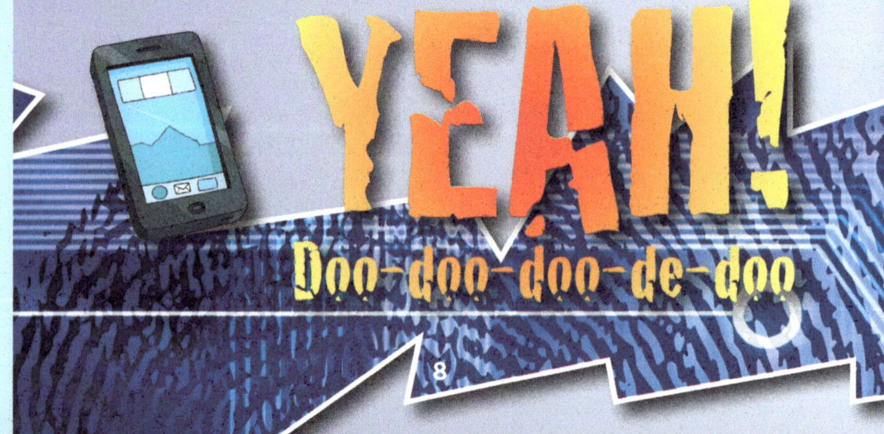

"Dwayne," insisted Shandy, her voice full of urgency, as she burst into the classroom. "I must examine the body before Janitor John receives notification of this."

Dwayne and Shandy hurriedly exchanged meaningful glances. The moment Janitor John was informed of a deceased goldfish in Room 7, he'd hurry to the classroom. This was, technically, his jurisdiction. A short flush later, the intrepid investigators would lose their victim forever.

"The victim's body," indicated Dwayne, "is over there."

Looking serious, Shandy advanced upon the bundle of damp tissues Dwayne had carefully placed on the nearest desk. She gingerly peeled off the tissues. Even after examining plenty of deceased goldfish during her investigative career, she still hated this moment. Steeling herself, she tried to remain professional.

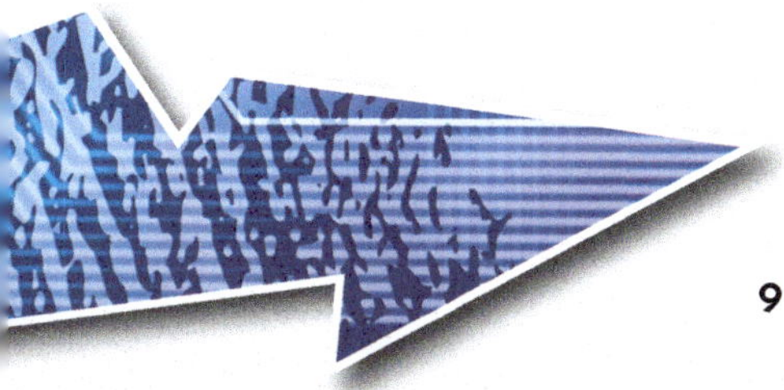

“Hmm,” she murmured, examining the victim for identification. “This is not just any goldfish,” she said with bated breath, “this is Flipper, the classroom’s resident goldfish.”

“Interesting,” grimaced Dwayne, shooting his assistant a sideways glance. “Everything is gradually coming together. The classroom, the upturned goldfish bowl, the lifeless goldfish. Now we have confirmation of our victim’s identity, only one nagging question remains unanswered.”

Wrapping Flipper in the tissues again, Shandy narrowed her eyes and focused on Dwayne, reading his thoughts. “Why?” she exclaimed with a look of steely determination.

“And who?” added Dwayne Pipe thoughtfully.

“That’s two questions,” said Shandy.

Whipping off his sunglasses, Dwayne looked dramatically at Shandy. “Correct,” he said.

Shandy looked at Dwayne, unable to disguise her admiration for his uncanny ability to summarise a situation instantly.

Dwayne and Shandy checked their text messages during Louden Clear's meticulous forensic examination. Louden was searching for conclusive clues, preferably ones directly identifying the criminal who had terminated Flipper's life so prematurely.

"Hmm," murmured Louden, extracting something unmistakeably suspicious with tweezers commandeered from his sister's make-up bag. "An interesting discovery."

"Criminals always leave a clue," said Shandy, with the voice of experience. "What's so interesting, Louden?"

"A hair, short and brown with grey flecks."

"An interestingly short, brown and grey-flecked hair," mused Dwayne, mulling over this new information. "Interesting because Janitor John always vacuums the classrooms every evening."

"The hair, therefore, belongs to someone who was present between yesterday afternoon and this morning," nodded Louden.

"Correct," murmured Dwayne. "That's the third question answered."

“We didn’t have a third question,” remarked Shandy, wondering what her clever colleague was thinking.

“We do now,” Dwayne replied, folding his sunglasses and placing them carefully in his shirt pocket. “When?”

Dwayne Pipe walked over to Flipper’s lifeless remains, encased in damp tissues. “You, my friend, are wrapped up ...”

Suddenly, the school bell’s shrieking drowned out the air conditioner’s purr. A crescendo of evidence-contaminating footsteps stampeded towards the classroom.

“But,” continued Dwayne, glancing downwards, “this investigation isn’t.”

CRIME SCENE INVESTIGATION CASE 379336

TIME:	0745 HOURS
LOCATION:	CLASSROOM 7
	GANDWILLI SCHOOL
VICTIM:	FLIPPER
PERPETRATOR:	UNIDENTIFIED

CRIME SCENE INVESTIGATION CASE 379336 CONTAINS EVIDENCE DO NOT TAMPER

2 Suspect Evidence

Barb Dwyer, the Room 7 teacher, peered into the cubbyhole beneath her desk drawer. Something was missing.

"Right!" she snapped angrily. She slowly looked around the roomful of alarmed expressions. "Has anyone taken my boiled-egg sandwich?"

Dwayne, Shandy and Louden snatched a furtive glance at each other.

"Give us a description, Miss Dwyer," suggested Dwayne, cocking his head to one side. Beneath the deceptively cool exterior, Dwayne's brain was whirring.

"It has two pieces of bread on either side," said Miss Dwyer, peering at Dwayne suspiciously. "In between, there is egg. Boiled egg."

"Make a note," whispered Dwayne to Louden. "We may need an artist's impression sketch."

CRIME SCENE INVESTIGATION CASE 379336

TIME:	0900 HOURS
LOCATION:	CLASSROOM 7
	GANDWILLI SCHOOL
SUBJECT:	MISSING EGG SANDWICH
NOTE:	ARTIST'S IMPRESSION ONLY, NOT ACTUAL SANDWICH

"Approximate age?" asked Dwayne, fixing Barb Dyer with an investigative eye.

"I'm twenty-two," confessed Miss Dwyer, shuffling uncomfortably. "OK. Twenty-three."

"The sandwich, Miss Dwyer," said Dwayne, polishing his sunglasses calmly. "I was referring to the missing sandwich."

Miss Dwyer's eyes flashed. Under interrogation, she knew that she'd slipped up. "A day old," she said. "I couldn't eat my lunch yesterday so I saved a sandwich for today."

Dwayne was about to continue Miss Dwyer's merciless interrogation when there was a knock on the classroom door and Janitor John entered. The janitor's lips involuntarily curled upwards when he noticed Miss Dwyer, plunging down again as he glowered at the students.

"I'm here for Flipper," he grunted.

"Here's Flipper," said Shandy softly. She reverently placed the small wad of tissues onto the dustpan that Janitor John held out.

"The sandwich was saved. But not the goldfish," mused Dwayne, ignoring the interruption to his questioning. "Is there something you're not telling us, Miss Dwyer?"

"OK. Twenty-five," admitted the teacher, eying Dwayne defiantly.

"I'll return," interrupted Janitor John, looking curiously at Barb Dwyer. "Return to clean up the goldfish bowl."

"And obliterate our forensic investigation," murmured Louden.

But Dwayne's calculating mind was elsewhere. Tapping a pencil on a piece of paper, his eyes flitted from Janitor John to Miss Dwyer and back again.

"What is it?" whispered Shandy.

"It," replied Dwayne evenly, "is a pencil. Two halves of wood, glued together with some graphite in-between. And," he said, turning to face Shandy, "an eraser on the top."

Shandy knew that when Dwayne was working on a complicated investigation, he was better left undisturbed. But Dwayne smiled, holding the pencil up triumphantly.

"It's also useful for recording evidence," he said. "And recording evidence," he added, taking some paper from his desk, "is exactly what I'm going to do."

At lunchtime, Dwayne, Shandy and Louden gathered beside the bike shed. Dwayne glanced around to check no prying eyes were watching. Then, satisfied they were not under surveillance, he pulled something from his pocket.

"What's that?" said Louden.

"That," replied Dwayne, "is my handkerchief. This," he said, rustling in his pocket and pulling out a folded piece of paper, "is evidence."

"Where did it come from?" asked Louden, trying to disguise his excitement.

"A pencil," answered Dwayne, slipping off his sunglasses and unfolding the paper.

"A what?" said Louden in surprise.

Sighing, Dwayne fixed Louden with a meaningful gaze.

"It's two halves of wood, glued together with some graphite in-between, and an eraser on the top."

He flipped the paper around so his colleagues could examine the evidence. Shandy and Louden studied the paper carefully.

"It's two heads," said Shandy finally. "Those round bits are heads."

"And the short spiky stuff on top is hair," concluded Louden. "You drew two heads with hair on top."

"Not just any heads with hair on top," said Dwayne, carefully folding the drawing again.

“The left-hand head represents Miss Dwyer. The right-hand head represents Janitor John.”

“And?” said Shandy.

“And,” explained Dwayne, “I’ve noticed something in common.”

“What’s that?” hissed Shandy, desperate to discover the connection between the suspects.

“It means a feature they both share,” murmured Dwayne.

“Yes, Dwayne, but what do they have in common?”

“It’s short and brown with grey flecks!”

“What is?” burst out Louden.

“Their hair,” breathed Dwayne emphatically.

Louden felt in his pocket for the small plastic container into which he’d dropped that morning’s clue. After staring at the single short, brown, grey-flecked hair with renewed interest, he nodded a confirmation.

“You mean ...?” gasped Shandy.

"I do," nodded Dwayne. "We're searching for a hairdresser who only cuts hair short, uses grey highlights on brown hair, has a deep-seated resentment of goldfish and who finds day-old boiled-egg sandwiches irresistible."

Shandy and Louden pondered this information.

"Or," said Shandy, "maybe it was just Miss Dwyer or Janitor John?"

"Maybe," conceded Dwayne reluctantly.

"But which suspect?" said Louden.

"Hmm," muttered Dwayne. "A fourth question. And this investigation has only answered one. You know what that means?" he said, looking down at the grass pensively.

Shandy and Louden held their breath.

"There are still three left."

3 A Conspiracy

"Miss Dwyer's holding something back," said Dwayne, looking at Shandy and Louden. "We need to put a tail on that suspect."

Shandy and Louden glanced at each other.

"Won't that hurt?" asked Louden.

"Not," replied Dwayne, "if that tail is a crime-scene investigator named Louden, following her around from a safe distance on his bicycle."

"Oh," said Louden. "I thought you meant a long, furry tail, like the one that possum's got," he said apologetically, pointing at a small marsupial nestled in the eucalyptus tree towering over the bike shed.

"No," smiled Dwayne. "I meant a tail like you, following her around from a safe distance on your bicycle."

"I'm on it," nodded Louden.

"No, you're not," pointed out Shandy, shaking her head. "Your bike's over there."

"I'll be on it the moment school finishes," clarified Louden.

"Follow Miss Dwyer's every move. I saw how she and Janitor John were looking at each other. Our suspect is being economical with the truth."

"You mean ..." gasped Shandy.

"Thirty," said Dwayne, putting his sunglasses back on. "Thirty, at least."

Back in the classroom, Dwayne spent the afternoon examining his recording of that morning's evidence. He studied the left-hand head, wondering what possible motive Miss Dwyer had for hiding her own boiled-egg sandwich. And Janitor John – why would he commit a heinous crime against an innocent goldfish?

"OK, it's time for maths," said Miss Dwyer, breaking in on Dwayne's attempts to unravel the criminal conundrum.

Putting the paper aside, he reached for his maths textbook. "It certainly is maths time," he whispered to himself. "Because there's something that's definitely not adding up."

Louden allowed himself a surreptitious look at his wristwatch. Five o'clock. This stake-out was interminable.

Upon arriving at the stake-out location, he'd cleverly concealed himself and his bicycle behind a convenient tree opposite Miss Dwyer's house. Everything seemed calm from the exterior – but Louden's investigative experience reminded him that appearances were deceptive. Miss Dwyer could at that very moment be sitting beneath a noticeboard plastered with gory pictures of goldfish fatalities, feverishly plotting another senseless goldfish massacre.

Suddenly, a car slowly heading towards Miss Dwyer's house interrupted Louden's thoughts. Its occupant switched off the engine. What could this disturbing and troublesome development mean? Did she have an accomplice?

Unaware that he was under surveillance, the figure opened the vehicle door and stood up. Louden gasped, instantly recognising Janitor John. Louden scrabbled in his pocket for his mobile telephone. He needed backup.

But, before he could compose an urgent message, a further complication arrived. Louden watched in amazement as another seemingly innocent car turned the corner and slowly pulled up outside Miss Dwyer's house.

He stifled another gasp as he identified the second car's driver. It was none other than the notorious Seymour Leggs, the school principal.

"A conspiracy," he whispered, observing Mr Leggs hitch up his shorts and pull his ankle socks high above his Roman sandals. "They are a gang!"

Dwayne pressed his mobile phone to his ear and listened carefully as Louden reported his alarming discovery. Then he stared into the distance.

"The fish gang has been fingered," he said slowly. "Tomorrow, Dwayne, we need to turn up the heat."

He turned back to the phone.

"We'll smoke them out. And they'll jump from the frying pan into the fire."

"They'll be gutted," predicted Louden.

"The scales of justice will see to that, my friend," murmured Dwayne. "The net is slowly closing in on this investigation's fin-ale."

The next day, following breakfast, Shandy unfolded the piece of paper Dwayne had asked Louden to deliver the night before. Her investigative equipment, gleaming and glinting, awaited. Before beginning, she carefully examined the instructions. Correct procedure was critical. The investigation couldn't afford any mistakes.

The digital timer blinked with a large red "3.00" and Shandy pressed the button.

After carefully dropping the egg into the pot of boiling water, she checked the artist's impression that Louden had expertly sketched alongside the instructions.

"Two pieces of bread on either side," read Shandy. "In between, there is egg. Boiled egg."

Constructing an exact decoy replica of this critical evidence was exacting work, demanding every ounce of concentration Shandy could muster.

Dwayne crept along the corridor towards Room 7, determined to find a suitable location for the decoy boiled-egg sandwich. Shandy had only seconds to spare between arriving at school and the school bell going off. In setting a trap for an unknown perpetrator, every second counted.

Dwayne pushed open Room 7's door. And then he stopped, his mouth opening in dismay. "We," he said, contemplating the scene, "are too late."

Shandy and Louden arrived within minutes of Dwayne's urgent text message.

"Let's get to work, crime-scene investigation team," ordered Dwayne in a determined voice.

"More short brown and grey hairs here," reported Louden, squeezing his tweezers together. He was crouched over a trail of slimy, chewed-up whiteboard-marker lids leading from Miss Dwyer's desk towards the bookshelf. "And a black one!" he said excitedly. He looked at the new clue closely.

"Sorry," he said. "False alarm. That's from my sister's eyebrows. She must have been plucking them with my forensic tweezers last night."

Dwayne and Shandy were examining the shredded paper strewn around Dwayne's desk.

"What are they?" asked Shandy.

Dwayne lowered his sunglasses and looked at the floor.

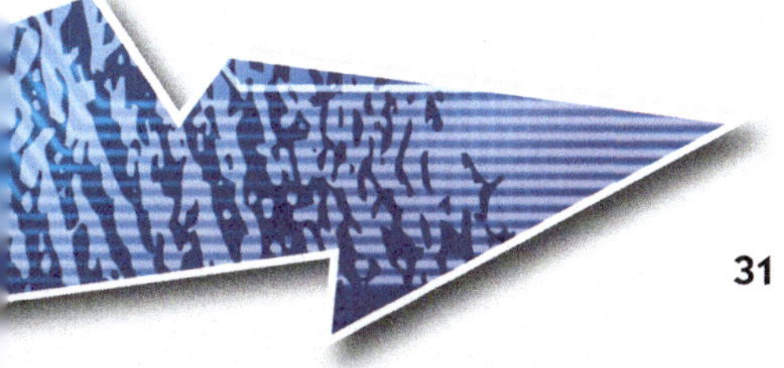

"This," he concluded, with the weary voice of a seasoned investigator, "is shredded paper strewn around my desk."

Upon having her suspicions confirmed, Shandy raised her eyebrows.

"But," continued Dwayne, "not just ordinary shredded paper strewn around my desk. This is shredded evidence strewn around my desk."

"Evidence?" asked Shandy. Dwayne unravelled one of the pieces of paper and Shandy gasped. The paper had a curving line with short, spiky stuff coming out the top.

"Your sketch of Miss Dwyer and Janitor John's heads!" she said.

"It *was* my sketch of Miss Dwyer and Janitor John's heads," corrected Dwayne. "Someone has attempted to destroy the evidence."

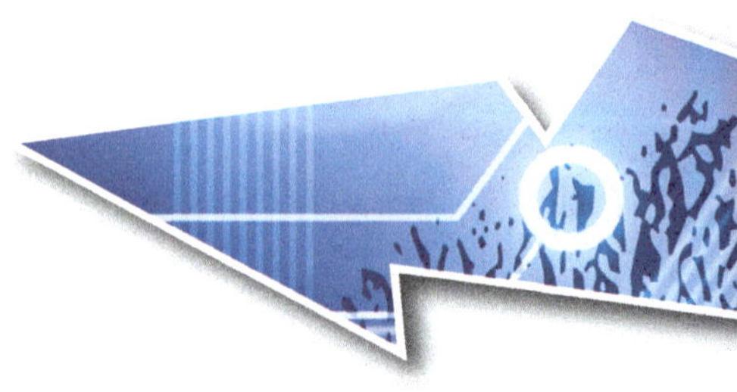

He whirled around.

"We need to go straight to the top," he continued. "We need to confront Principal Leggs."

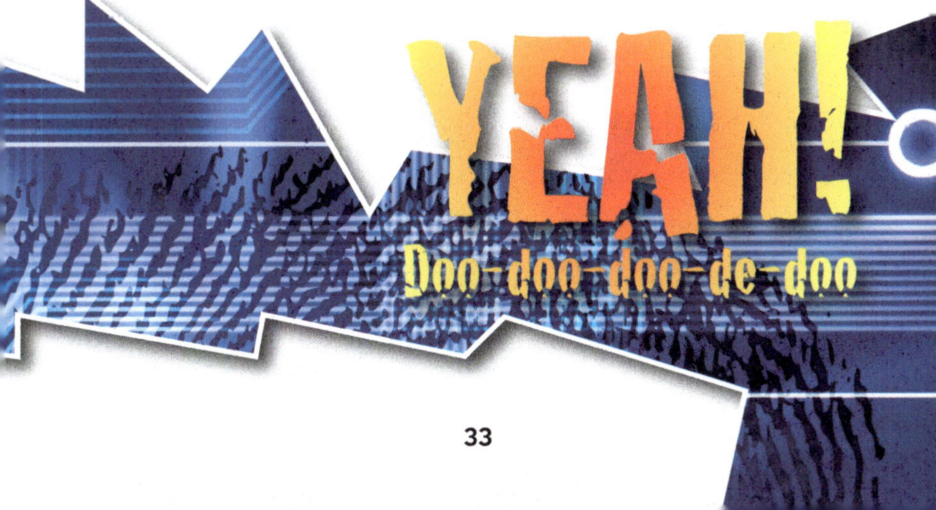

4 The Plot Thickens

"Where were you between the hours of five o'clock and seven-thirty last night?" quizzed Dwayne. He cocked his head sideways and gazed calmly at Principal Seymour Leggs.

"Out," spluttered the principal.

Dwayne sighed. "OK. You want to play hard ball? Let's play hard ball."

Mr Leggs looked bewildered. Dwayne calmly fixed him with an incisive eye.

"Are you or are you not carrying on a secret relationship with a mystery hairdresser who only cuts hair short, uses grey highlights on brown hair, has a deep-seated resentment of goldfish, finds day-old boiled-egg sandwiches irresistible and has a curious taste for sucking on whiteboard-marker lids and tearing up really good pictures of people's heads?"

Principal Leggs considered his response.

"Answer the question!" demanded Dwayne forcefully. "Yes or no!"

"No," denied Principal Leggs emphatically.

"Hmm," said Dwayne slowly. "My suspicions are confirmed." He looked at Shandy and Louden. "Our case is blown."

"Not so fast, Principal Leggs," said Louden, refusing to admit defeat. "I suppose you're also going to emphatically deny being at Miss Dwyer's house between five and seven-thirty?"

"No," admitted Principal Leggs. "I was there."

Dwayne, Shandy and Louden looked at each other triumphantly. And then Principal Leggs brought their entire goldfish-slaughtering gang conspiracy tumbling down.

"It was her birthday party. She turned forty."

A stunned silence pervaded the principal's office as Shandy and Louden stared at Dwayne, Principal Leggs stared at Dwayne, Shandy and Louden, and Dwayne removed his sunglasses and stared at the floor.

"Forty?" he murmured to himself. "How could you be so wrong?"

"Our crime-scene investigation is missing something," said Shandy.

"The answer is here," said Dwayne confidently. "We just need to find it.

Dwayne, Shandy and Louden had returned to the classroom crime scene. Dwayne set a chair beside the bookcase, looking grimly at the shelves above. He pulled at a shelf.

"Excellent," he said. "This bookcase is firmly fixed to the wall and, unless I'm mistaken, these shelves are firmly fixed to the bookcase."

"What are you going to do?" asked Louden, considering whether or not to remind Dwayne that very recently he had, in fact, been mistaken.

"I," replied Dwayne, clambering onto the chair, "am going to get to the bottom of this."

"How?" said Shandy.

"I am getting to the bottom of this," replied Dwayne, pushing his sunglasses up his nose, "by getting to the top of this."

"Clever," said Shandy. "But be careful. That's dangerous!"

From his precarious vantage point, Dwayne stretched one foot towards the shelf in the bookcase where the recently deceased Flipper had once blithely swum, unaware of the ghastly fate that awaited. Grateful for his expert training in bookcase climbing, Dwayne hauled himself up towards the uppermost shelf.

"Be careful, Dwayne," said Louden.

"What's there?" said Shandy, knowing that Dwayne wouldn't allow an increase in altitude to compromise his investigation skills.

"I see," came Dwayne's muffled voice, "a biscuit wrapper."

Reaching up, past the biscuit wrapper, he rattled the grid covering the air conditioner. It swung open, and Shandy and Louden looked at each other.

"And this air conditioner grid," confirmed Dwayne, "has been left wide open." He glanced down at Shandy and Louden. "Just like our investigation."

After clambering down, Dwayne rubbed his hands together. "We've discovered how our perpetrator entered the premises. The perpetrator came straight through the air conditioning vent."

Shandy stared at the air conditioner grate, swinging open over a hole no bigger than a sheet of paper.

"But who could fit through that?" she said, furrowing her brow and trying to make sense of this critical breakthrough. "It's far too small for Miss Dwyer," she said, "and certainly too small for Janitor John."

Dwayne slipped off his sunglasses and polished the lenses with his handkerchief.

"The question is not 'who'," he declared decisively. "The question is 'what?'"

"No!" exclaimed Shandy, who knew exactly what that meant.

"Yes," replied Dwayne, twitching his head. "That, my friends, is the fifth question!"

Janitor John, having been cleared of suspicion in the case of the deceased goldfish, was only too eager to assist the investigation. He, too, wanted to discover who was responsible for this mysterious series of events.

“Is the trap ready?” whispered Dwayne. The sun was setting, and eerie shadows were lengthening across the classroom carpet.

Janitor John nodded, his focus on the air conditioner above the bookcase.

Seymour Leggs and Barb Dwyer were crouched in one corner of the room while Dwayne, Shandy and Louden were huddled in the other, ready for the dramatic conclusion of this investigation.

Together, they huddled and crouched, then crouched and huddled, while the tension rose and the sun sank. Finally, the sun disappeared over the horizon, and with it, the last of the daylight and the feeling in Seymour Legg’s right foot. Dwayne removed his sunglasses for what he thoroughly expected to be the final time that evening.

His fingers felt the long piece of string that he held tightly. Everything rested upon Janitor John’s trap – and the piece of birthday cake that the team had confiscated from a reluctant Miss Dwyer earlier that afternoon.

Suddenly, the silence in the gloomy classroom was broken by a scrabbling sound. The tension in Room 7 skyrocketed. Everyone's eyes remained firmly riveted to the air conditioner.

Then they saw it. A pair of glinting eyes were reflected in the final seconds of the blood-red sunset outside the building.

"Wait for it!" breathed Dwayne, his fingers closing around the string.

Then he tugged on the string and a cacophony of screaming filled the air. There was a crash, a groan from the principal who was rubbing the circulation back into his foot, and then silence.

"Busted!" accused Dwayne, slowly rising from his hiding position and confronting the perpetrator. "You're going behind bars!"

5 Guilty!

"Actually," said Janitor John, peering at the perpetrator, "we can't hold him. This perp's got immunity. I'm only authorised to take him fifty metres away."

"The law," said Dwayne wisely, "protects the guilty and the innocent. Thankfully, Gandwilli's goldfish population can sleep soundly, knowing this perpetrator is behind bars tonight."

Shandy stared at the beady eyes looking out from the stainless-steel cage. "I'm sure he didn't mean to do it," she said. "He probably just slipped while climbing down the bookcase, looking for food."

"The temptation of a boiled-egg sandwich, filling the room with its distinctive aroma. A faulty air conditioning grate. A foolhardy climb. A falling claw desperately catching the edge of a goldfish bowl." Dwayne stared at everyone. "All of them inconsequential, random acts that mean little."

He sighed and flicked his eyes towards the empty space where the goldfish bowl had sat. “Except for Flipper.”

The captive possum scratched its rear leg and a shower of brown hairs, flecked with grey, floated onto the carpet.

“Bother,” said Janitor John vehemently.

Miss Dwyer put her arm around John’s shoulder. “I know what you’re thinking,” she comforted him. “What a waste of a perfectly innocent goldfish.”

“Nope,” murmured Janitor John. “I was thinking I’ve just done the vacuuming and now look at that carpet.” The janitor shook his head in resignation. “I’ll take this little fellow into the bush behind the school and let him go,” he said. “And then I’ll return with my ladder and some screws to repair that air conditioning grate.”

“A few twists of the screwdriver,” said Dwayne with a meaningful look, “would have saved all the twists in this sorry episode.”

Later that night, Dwayne sat alone at the kitchen table, turning the pages of the local paper. He was thinking about the case when an advertisement caught his eye.

"Hair too long?" it read. "Tired of boring brown? Need a few highlights? Why not book in for a cut and dye tomorrow?"

It was an advertisement for a new hairdresser who had just arrived in town.

Dwayne closed the paper and looked out the window.

"Hair today, dye tomorrow," he said. "That's a fine epitaph that won't be used for any more innocent goldfish," he nodded.

He took off his sunglasses and polished them vigorously. "Not on my watch."

CLIENT
CEN

JOB CODE
LP021529

QUANTITY
100 copies

ISBN / ITEM CODE
9780170217552

TYPE
Book

TITLE
NLD 5 F L15 CSI Classroom

TEXT PRINTING

Print By	18/10/2023
Stock	CVG Silk (115 gsm)
Extent	48 pages
Sheet Size	215 x 268
Machine	Ricoh C9210
Colours	colour
Bleed	Yes

COVER PRINTING

Print By	18/10/2023
Stock	1_Sided_Artboard (230 gsm)
Sheet Size	482 x 330
Machine	Ricoh C9210
Colours	colour
Bleed	Yes
Duplex	Yes
Laminate	Gloss
Jacket	None

FINISHING

Bind Style	Perfect Bound
Trim Size	198 x 129 mm
Spine	2.8 mm

FOR ORDERS (1)

Order	Destination	Item Details	Required By
CEN-ORD-000-7P3 (A01055759)	TOLL – C/O Cengage 16 Hollinsworth Road MARSDEN PARK NSW 2765	100 copies	19/10/2023

CEN: Cengage
Job Released at 17:50 PM on Wed 11/10/23
Intent 1011 / Riverwood Workflow 332:
Medium Book, Cover; Text C9210